Flint And Steel

Flint And Steel

A STORY OF SURVIVAL

JOHN WEISHAAR, ED. D.

Library of Congress Control Number: 2011902070
ISBN: Hardcover   978-1-4568-6678-5
                 Softcover   978-1-4568-6677-8
                 Ebook   978-1-4568-6679-2

To order additional copies of this book, contact:
Xlibris Corporation
1-888-795-4274
www.Xlibris.com
Orders@Xlibris.com
94016

ACKNOWLEDGEMENTS AND THANKS

To wife Cla for her support while living in the Alaskan wilderness, encouragement, life long companionship, and love

To son Keith for his experiences and support while living in the Alaskan wilderness

To son Eric for his encouragement to get the book written

To Laura Stiles for her continued encouragement to finish the book and support

To John Flink—Contributing Editor and his incredible creative writing ability

Lannon Heflin—Cover Design and great friendship

CHAPTER I

"I went to the woods because I wished to live deliberately,
to front only the essential facts of life, and see if
I could learn what it had to teach, and not, when
I came to die, discover that I had not lived."

Henry David Thoreau

The world was still, silent and forever. The hoarse breath of wind across the plain of snow took on the qualities of a deafening, coarse silence. Ryan Larsen was frozen with it. He reminded himself to breathe out and felt his stomach and ribs quiver. The frozen grip of shock was beginning to thaw from his muscles and mind and he started to take stock of the situation.

The snow beneath him was sagging gently. A sharp, hollow cracking came from all around him as though he were standing on a giant amplifier. But it was the ice of a pond, frozen over and hidden by snow that now complained beneath him. Anything larger than his 120 pound frame would have already plunged through the fragile surface, he knew. But that thought was little comfort for him, as he also knew that to stand still, to step forward, or to step back could still yield the same fate for him.

"Slowly, slowly," he whispered to himself when he found control of his motions and thoughts.

As though responding, a deafening crack from the ice split the air. A flock of birds lifted away, as though too scared to watch what would happen to the fourteen year old. He suddenly felt more alone than before. Now he was the last living thing on the landscape, the last blemish for the unforgiving, desolate wilderness to stamp out.

His fear was growing. He closed his eyes, hoping to open them and find himself anywhere else. Anywhere else in the world. But he knew that when he opened them, almost cruelly, he would find himself as alone as before. Nowhere else in the world existed right now. No one else was alive. It was just Ryan, the frozen lake, and his will to survive.

Moments before—an age that now seemed like a lifetime ago—Ryan had decided to tramp a shortcut across a meadow. He was making good time through the spruce timberland of the Alaskan north country on one of the days that only seemed to get as bright as the last moments of dusk in his Texas hometown. Even with that little bit of light fading, he had decided to push on further through the monotonous, peaceful snow country.

Ryan Larsen exhaled slowly, feeling his stomach and ribs tremble. He remembered back to what seemed like a lifetime ago when he took in his last breath. In his panic he had seen the world around him as unfair, vindictive. Now—as the panic waned and hopelessness filled its place—he realized that nature is a place with neither rewards nor punishments, just consequences.

Consequences . . .

Thin ice, he thought to himself, eyes still closed.

Consequences . . .

Stay on top and I will live.

Consequences . . .

Fall through and I will die.

Consequences . . .

I strayed from the trees, I took a shortcut, and now I am in danger.

This wasn't helping.

Consequences . . .

My mother and father when I don't return.

This wasn't helping at all.

It is a fact that a momentary wandering of attention out here can have catastrophic results. He was not unprepared for the journey: He had snowshoes on his feet; he had a compass, map, hatchet, fire-starting equipment, and rope in his bag and—most importantly—the knowledge how to use all of them to ensure his survival. His father had taught him how to use all of it expertly.

Of course, his father had taught him to read terrain also. Ryan knew to look for tell-tale signs of what lay beneath a layer of snow: trees, grass sticking out, jagged protrusions of rock, frozen remnants of vegetation and uneven ground all suggested firm footing beneath. But the long slow sagging of a shallow bowl, a flat area with a weighed down depression in the center betrayed an ice-gilded pond.

This faux-ground is on what he now stood. Moments before, when he strayed from the ridge of trees, he failed to notice that his signs were disappearing one by one. He was thinking only of putting the most distance between the drop-off point at which his parents had left him early that same day and where he would stop to build shelter for the night. It was his coming of age adventure: a day's hike into the wilderness to nowhere in particular, the building of a temporary shelter and fire, and two days of the barest survival against the rawest of elements: February in the Alaskan Wilderness. Ryan felt that to become a man one should solitarily face the wilderness, not to conquer it, but to realize his own limitations and overcome any obstacles possible. It was the ritual of passing from boyhood to manhood. A time of reflection about self and how we need to co-exist in nature under her rules.

Now, though, every step he had taken in haste to enter that solitude was a step that left him more alone, with less hope of being rescued than the step before. The Alaskan wilderness is so desolate that, were it physically possible to do so, he could scream for several days without anyone noticing. He wished his mother and father were there right then. He willed his father's voice to reach him through the forested mountains, to tell him what to do.

His father's voice never came. Ryan was alone. He was, of course, because he had planned it that way.

He looked down at his feet. The thick, insulated boots were strapped securely into the snowshoes. He patted his gloved hands against his arms to make sure he still had the last tool he ever wanted or expected to have to use out here.

"Well," he said aloud, "guess there's no point in waiting to live or die. Time to get on with it." His heart pounded with the dumping of excess adrenaline.

He crouched low to the ground to make his preparations.

As if by response, the wilderness around him became animated. A wolf howled in the distance, a gust of wind slid across the land and the frozen lake beneath him menacingly creaked out a warning.

His quest had begun.

CHAPTER II

"I think I could turn and live with the animals, they are so placid and self-contained."

Walt Whitman (American Poet)

There was no easy way to tell whether to step forward or back. Ryan scanned all around him. In each direction he could see trees and hills, but nothing to tell him immediately whether he was at the beginning of a small lake, or the middle of a decent-sized pond. He looked behind him and followed his footsteps visually, trying to pick out the point that the frozen over body of water began. It was possible that it was quite a bit back, that he had been trekking along so blindly certain that he didn't notice he was on ice until it was dangerously obvious. It was also possible that if the ice broke he would only find himself knee-deep in water, though that was very unlikely—and could still be ultimately deadly in these conditions.

"Better deal with what I'm certain about, then," he said aloud.

"The lighter I am, the less likely I am to fall through."

He let his pack slide off his shoulders. He placed it gingerly on the ice beside him. He unslung his rifle and laid that down, too.

"But these need to come with me."

He slipped a 25-foot length of parachute cord out of his bag. One end he hooked to his jacket with a carabineer, the other he looped through a harness strap on his bag and through the finger guard on the .22. He hooked and unhooked the carabineer several times to make sure that, if his bag happened to fall through, he could detach himself quickly so that it wouldn't pull him along with it.

He carefully unstrapped one foot from the snow shoe, then the other. He tied them onto his backpack.

"Now, I'm gonna move slowly backwards. It's held me this far, hopefully it'll hold me back."

He took his first little step. He wasn't sure how long he had been stopped for, but it must have been longer than he had thought. The cold had crept into his legs and his knees barely worked as a hinge. It had that hot and tired feeling of falling asleep from too long in one position. The leg went down with too much force, too clumsily. And where it did, he felt the ice give way. Like an actor falling partway through the floor of a stage, he felt his left leg slide all the way down through the ice and into the depths below.

"Oh, oh," he whimpered. He knew it was the start of something very bad.

Getting anything wet here could carry with it a death sentence, or at the very least a near-certainty of frostbite or worse. He found himself uncomfortably on all fours. Now that his left leg was thigh deep in water, Ryan was as good as trapped.

This wasn't how he wanted to be. It was awkward. When he started to pull with his arms, for some reason he had the mental image of wet ice-cubes falling through pieces of dissolving tissue. Instead of pulling his leg out, he lurched against the ice just below his hip, crumbling more of the barrier between himself and death. With each pull more ice beneath him gave way. He was like a Coast Guard icebreaker, rising up and inching forward, then breaking down and through the ice ahead. The water was soaking up his leg.

He was filled with panic and dread.

He was not in control as he sank further into the water.

Ryan was in shock. The ice was simultaneously breaking more in front of the boy, and freezing beside him. Nordic quick sand.

"Pull," he cried to himself. "Pull." He knew that this is how it happened in nature. You lose control of one thing, then another, then they start piling up. A tragic chain of errors.

He reached forward and all the ice beneath him was suddenly gone. He tried to hold his hands up so that he could at least resurface in the same hole. People don't always. Sometimes they become trapped, pushing up with all their might against the ice from one side, and the entirety of the earth and air pushing down on it from the other.

Ryan felt something experienced by far more dead men than living: water on the cusp of freezing oozing through his wool pants and coat. Slipping like fingers through his collar and down his back. Wrapping like a blanket of bitter snow around his face and head.

He bobbed back to the surface like a dead man. His face was uncovered, but his chest constricted, keeping him from breathing. He tried to gasp. His teeth chattered uncontrollably and his muscles contracted in shivers. For a long moment he couldn't breathe until he felt himself start to sink back under. Then he kicked with stiff legs and swept his arms in front of him to try and stay afloat. These actions seemed to loosen his chest and he was able to pull in a long breath, though the trembling continued.

"Now . . ." he whimpered, not knowing what to do next.

In his mind he saw a countdown clock. It was counting backward from ninety. There was no reason for him to see this, but he did. And he believed that he would be dead if he wasn't free from the water in that amount of time.

There was one piece of equipment that he had never practiced using. It was one that his father said he should pray never to use, but—if he ever did have to use it—would be the only thing to keep him alive. Just before leaving he had unscrewed two of the wooden legs from the underneath of an old couch. The cylinders of wood fit perfectly in Ryan's hands and each had a screw that extended from it about two inches. His dad had filed the screws down to sharp points for gripping ice, then attached each with a long piece of cord on the inside of his jacket. He had put them on and thought of a kindergartner stringing his mittens together through the arms of his coat to not forget them. They were like small ice picks dangling out the end of each sleeve on his coat.

Now he wriggled while splashing water into his face. Ryan pushed the dowels down until he gripped them in his mitten covered hands.

Sixty seconds.

He pushed himself to the ice bank and plunged the length of both pieces of metal into the ice, hoping that the action wouldn't just break more ice free. They held. He pulled with all of his might but wouldn't budge.

Forty-five seconds.

His legs might as well have been part of the lake—he couldn't feel them. He wrenched again at the fashioned ice-picks and tried to pull himself onto the ice. This time he did what he hoped would make both legs kick at the water. He felt himself rise partway up on the ice.

Twenty-five seconds.

He stretched one arm and dug the pick into the ice further up, then performed the same motions with the other.

Fifteen seconds.

With another pull he looked back and saw his boots and legs fully up on the ice. Without celebrating he turned his gaze in front of him. Fifty yards ahead of him he saw a group of spruce trees huddled together. It was the closest thing that promised solid ground beneath it.

The clock in his head reset to twenty minutes. He had to get to the trees and build a fire in twenty minutes. There was no other option for survival.

CHAPTER III

*"Come forth into the light of things.
Let Nature be your teacher."*

*William Wadsworth
(English romantic poet)*

The hardest and most strenuous task Ryan had ever completed in his life lay behind him. It marked, however, less than the halfway point of what he would need to go through if he were to survive. He was babbling to himself as he pulled, but he may as well have been mute. His words meant nothing. His eyes never left the thicket situated in front of them. After several feet, the slack pulled taught on the parachute chord and his pack, rifle and snowshoes began to lurch and slide after him with each pull of his arms. If he noticed the fine sheen of ice that crinkled, broke and reformed over the hinges of his arms and legs, he paid no attention to them, knowing they didn't matter.

What mattered was the goal ahead of him and his ability to get there, gather materials and start a fire before his blood became too viscous to run his veins. His motions were all automatic, necessary and would hopefully prove to be fruitful.

Halfway to the trees he felt strong enough to push himself up onto his knees. He twisted and put one boot flat on the snow. With supreme effort, Ryan pushed his hand against his bent knee and forced himself bipedal. His footsteps had the slow, fluid quality of video shot in slow motion. Left. Then right. Left. Then right. He was covering more ground this way than crawling. His waist was locked at thirty degrees, as though he were walking into a wind.

By the time he reached the trees, he was just as tired from the constant shivering as he was from the walk. He fell on his side and grasped for the rope connecting his pack—he needed it immediately. He could feel that his hairs poking out from his cap were frozen to his neck. His wool cap was probably frozen, too, for that matter. Tiny drops of water had formed icicled on his eyelashes.

Luckily there was no wind to fight against. He had built fires in it before, but wasn't sure he would be able to now. His father had taught him various ways to light a fire and all without matches or lighters. He had practiced over and over using friction from sticks, sparks from flints and the prongs of a nine-volt with some fine steel wool. But that was down in Texas when he never really needed a fire, anyway. Or, at least most of the time.

Here it was different. He had less than ten minutes before his shivering would have sapped too much energy, before he would stop thinking with whatever rationale remained within him and before the shivering was so bad that he could not even strike a match. The rules, the process for starting a fire were the same, but far more imperative here.

He fumbled the top of the bag open. There, right on top, was a purple, waterproof baggie. It held the most important contents of his entire bag and the only one that—when needed, like now—needed to be immediately available. That was why it was on the top. Under stress the mind becomes clouded and unsure of itself and the decisions it makes. Priority items need to be easily accessible and color coded for easy identification.

A dead spruce lay next on its side an arm's length from Ryan. The myriad branches in the air were brown and clogged with debris caught out of the Alaskan wind sometime since the tree had fallen. All of the debris was very dry.

Ryan reached out and pulled handfuls of the debris toward him. Then he broke several small twigs from the branches, and finally entire, wrist-sized branches. On his knees he slowly pulled at the snow in front of him. If there was too much piled up around the fire it could melt and suffocate the flames. He cleared an area flat enough the allow all the room a fire would need.

The contents of the purple bag weren't the only things with which Ryan could start a fire, but they were the ones that were needed to start a fire fast. There were two cotton balls smeared with Vasoline petroleum jelly, cotton lint of various sizes from the dryer and a small piece of a hacksaw blade connected to a piece of flint by a leather shoe-string.

He would need to be able to blow on the fire right when it began. If he didn't, it was likely that all the accelerant would be burned off and he would be left to have to make a fire the long and hard way—which he neither had the time nor the energy to do.

Beside the pile of debris, he laid down a few slabs of bark. Then he pulled the cotton balls apart and spread them on the sheets. He looked long at the flint and steel before picking them up in mitten covered hands. The first few strikes he took along the flint lacked the speed and force to cause enough spark-creating friction. He would have dropped the steel blade to the ground, had it not been connected by the piece of leather string. The steel part of the firestarter was a 2-inch piece of hardened hacksaw blade and the flint was saddled in a 3-inch long stick of magnesium.

"Here we go, here we go," he whispered to himself.

A brilliant spark flew from the tool. Ryan shrieked out with the delight of a primitive at the sight. He hit it again, again. Finally the cotton flared to life. Ryan pulled his snowy mittens off in his mouth and reached down to the debris pile. He fed on the lint, and then some grass and dry spruce needles, leaning close and breathing more life into the fire with each new deposit. Soon the flames grew.

"Fire is warmth is survival," he repeated several times as he began stacking the twigs and watching them ignite.

By the time he was stacking the thicker, arm's length branches in a teepee around the fire, he was turning a lucky corner from peril to a chance at living.

The zipper of his jacket was frozen. Ryan reached for the oblong slider tag and found it impossible to extricate from the teeth of the zipper. Even with the fire, the sub-freezing temperature and soaking clothes on him would kill him in less than an hour more. Hypothermia is the insidious killer of the outdoors.

He leaned close to the fire, hoping that he wouldn't burn himself. The flames were hot on his face and neck. After a moment he wrenched at the tag again, and pulled it down, releasing himself from the jacket. He noticed that the back of the coat was frozen as though the round of his back were still inside. He hung his jacket and shirt on a branch over the fire where they could dry.

"Now my pants," he whispered. He was still shaking, but the warmth from the fire on his skin was starting to have a positive affect.

The pants clung to his legs, but it wasn't until they were half way off that he started having trouble. No matter how he pushed, they were stuck.

"The boots," he realized, looking down. "My feet. When was the last time I felt them?"

They had gone past the point of sensation. Feet with frostbite could become disfigured, discolored permanently numb, or, worse, potentially face amputation.

"No," he cried, pulling the laces of the boots. He unstrung each eyehole, wanting to treat his feet as gingerly as possible. Just because he couldn't feel them didn't mean he wouldn't cause them potentially more damage if he tried to just rip his feet out.

Eventually the boots fell away. He gritted his teeth as he stripped the socks off his feet. Neither looked any different than before. Perhaps they would be alright. He tried to curl in his toes. None moved. He could roll at the ankle, but nothing below.

He leaned forward until his hands felt warm, but not hot. There he placed a branch and then placed his feet above the branch. If he put them too far in, they would burn without his knowing it.

Soon feeling began to bloom in his feet. He was pleased to feel them, to know that he had not lost all feeling, but a moment later the sensations were shooting with blunt, mute pain. His entire foot hurt as it passed through the thawing process.

He laid back and squeezed his eyes shut. Without the wind he was able to gain heat by sitting close to the flames, even without his outer garments.

As he closed his eyes and growled through gritted teeth against the pain, he began to formulate his next steps in his mind. It was always important to have next steps—especially when in the wild with night about to fall.

CHAPTER IV

"The Wilderness holds answers to questions man
has not yet learned how to ask."

Nancy Newhall
(American photography critic)

Ryan was wrapped in his sleeping bag, finally resting a few feet from the fire. Every so often he had to add another log onto it. He had warmed so much that he had twice taken short trips from the heat of the fire to gather more wood to put on it. The first time hadn't been for long—less than an armful of timber that required him to move less than ten feet from the fire. The second time was a bit more substantial. On that trip he gathered a hefty armful of kindling that he was certain would last him through the night.

Not that he planned to rely just on the pile for survival. His father had drilled into him the general rules of three for living outdoors: a human can usually go three minutes without air, three hours without warmth and shelter in extreme conditions, three days without water and three weeks without food. The key is to keep them in order of priority. The air wasn't a problem—at least not since he pulled himself out of that ice trap. But if he didn't build some shelter, if he went to sleep staring at the fire—which he could feel himself inclined to do—he could find himself a victim of wind, snow or other elements.

He took another moment to admire the brilliance of the fire. It snapped and hissed with the rhythm of speech, and the flames gyrated like a dancer in the night. It was because of fire that he was alive. He thought back to the dumb excitement he felt when the first sparks had erupted and realized what an amazing thing fire is. And what an absolving presence as well. At its worst, its most painful, the fire will turn on stupid mistakes and destroy them. But at its best—which it was at for him—it rescued him from another careless mistake.

He tossed another piece of branch on the fire and watched the embers at the base explode into the air like lightning bugs taking flight. The fire was a calming presence bringing back sanity. Without it he would have been in this barren, foreign wilderness without much hope. But fire was a friend that gave him accompaniment and warmth.

But it alone was not enough. Exposed to everything around them, both Ryan and the fire could be snuffed out within minutes. Life without protection in the wild was too tenuous to assume. He needed stronger protection, insulation, a peaceful barrier between him and everything outside.

His clothes were now dry. The fire had left them warm and musty with smoke. He pulled them back on and found a sincere appreciation for how the thick wool of his clothing reflected the heat back upon him that he generated. It was time to find shelter.

There were no natural formations nearby that would be useful. Plus, it wouldn't be wise to leave the fire. The way he saw it was that he had a few options. Building a snow cave was the first one. He and his father had built one as a matter of know-how two weeks before. When done well, they provide the best shelter. But with one person building it the strenuous labor would certainly soak Ryan's clothes with sweat. He didn't think that he could put out that sort of energy after the day he had. The second option was to build a lean-to shelter. He had a hatchet and a knife, and good amounts of rope. But how long would it take? They were simple enough, but darkness was setting in, and Ryan would have to be selective in what materials he chose if it was going to be worthwhile, and he didn't have enough time left before it would be too dark. Finally, he could build a snow trench. It was the most rudimentary, but also made the most sense.

He looked at the GI shovel folded up in his pack. When opened, it was little more than a spade, but the hard and sharp edge would break through the snow and ice nicely. It would only need to be slightly longer than he was tall and only two feet deep. This would allow him to fit completely and comfortably inside and to be protected from everything outside.

A half hour after the decision was made the trench was dug. In the last remnants of sunlight, Ryan cut several large spruce boughs from a nearby tree. He carried back the giant, palm-like growths. Though he had dug two feet down in the snow, he would still be surrounded by snow on all sides. The boughs below him would provide separation from the heat-siphoning cold while ones above him would shelter him from snow. Snow caves and snow trenches if properly constructed are good insulators in cold temperatures.

Snow? He hadn't cared to notice before, but he now realized it was snowing. It was just a small amount, even though it had been completely unpredicted by the latest weather reports he heard over the radio just before leaving his home that day.

"These branches are more than just precautionary now," Ryan thought as he pulled them over him like a down-filled comforter on his bed at home.

In his fashioned shelter he began to take stock of his inventory. Especially of his food. He was hungry, but had only brought enough food for three days. He stumbled across a brownie his mom must have put in his bag. It seemed like a good idea to save it until it was more of a necessity. He was so tired he just wanted to sleep. He felt like he had just run a marathon.

He thought of everything he'd been through. He was hiking and carrying that pack for a long time before even falling through the ice—just that alone should have made him famished enough to want a feast. Then there was all that shivering. How many calories had he burned contracting all of his muscles and chattering away at his teeth? And what had his body burned in an attempt to stay warm before? And gathering the wood? Digging the trench?

"Being stranded out here isn't a reason to not eat. Just the opposite in fact."

In two days he would be back to the pick-up point where his dad had dropped him to discover himself in the wilderness. He would just have to ration his food until then. But without food, now, he wouldn't be able to think, reason, or generate heat. And if something happened that required a surge of energy, he would never be able to pass the test without some food.

But first he would eat some more wholesome foods. He opened a can of beans and leaned them against the fire, tore of a hunk of bread from the home-baked loaf, and pulled apart a large serving of moose jerky. It was a camp-side feast. His belly was satisfied.

At the end of it all, he decided his mother's brownie was a good way to reward himself for staying alive. Though he wasn't sure that after his mindless mistake he deserved a reward. A couple of times he had begun to think about what would have happened had he not been able to pull himself out of the water, or start the fire in time . . . Quickly dismissed!! It was too scary to think about.

"It was just a degree from greatness," he said to himself, snapping out of a morbid thought. "Had I just paid attention I would be getting on without a hitch. And, anyway, I saved myself from the danger." Simultaneously, he was thinking of himself and his mom and dad at the same time.

His belly was full. Surprisingly, his mind was less tired than his body now. Before they were both exhausted. But now he felt sharp, but tired mentally, instead of his mind being both dull and exhausted. Physically he was tired just the same, but sleep would cure that. The mind is regenerated when rested.

He imagined in two days telling them the story. Ha! His father was a native of these parts and had experiences like these that he still talks about. When his father had taught him about shelter building and survival, Ryan was just a Texas kid out having fun. It was akin to learning to pull a parachute rip cord without jumping out of a plane the first time. But now he had the danger around him and was applying the learning. He thought about his mom, too. He might have to wait until she wasn't around to tell parts of the experience. Sometimes she got that look when she was disappointed, scared. She was just barely agreeable to letting the family move up there. One wrong thing like this might send her packing back to the Lone Star State. The family moved to the wilderness to live the life written by Henry David Thoreau. He remembers his dad quoting Thoreau, " . . . . to live deliberately, facing the essential things in life, and learning the lessons it has to teach." He smiled sleepily when he imagined what she would yell at his father: "I'm going back with or without you!" But Ryan knew he wouldn't have a choice. She would take him back to those dusty, hot plains. He was drifting back, and could almost see the sunset over the scorched prairie of the Hill Country.

Inside the little home, Ryan drifted to sleep. Snow drifted down from the heavens and slowly started snubbing the fire out. Soon the glow barely cast any more light on the trees in the little thicket. Moments later, a pair of eyes watched as the last embers of heat suffocated. Visitors unexpected!!!! Imagination or reality?

CHAPTER V

*"Generally speaking, a howling wilderness does not howl; it
is the imagination of the traveler that does the howling."*

Henry David Thoreau

Ryan slept comfortably enough. He always found the contrast between the cold of the air on his face and the warmth of the rest of his body in a sleeping bag to induce a particularly calm, heavy sleep. But when it came to waking in the morning, it was a test of wills to get moving. The tensions of stress cause stiffness and aches.

To his surprise, the snow had woven a silky sheen over everything. It wasn't much, but it was there and still continuing to fall lightly. He peered into the horizon and watched the flakes fall as though one entity across the entire meadow. Between the dinner and the night's rest, he found himself feeling more prepared to deal with being out in the wild.

He unzipped the sleeping bag and slipped out. He had further insulated himself with clothing and his hat and mittens.

Luckily the fire he had built the night before had protected a few hot coals within its center. He cleared the charred remains of the logs from above the coals and was soon making loose piles of twigs and dried grasses to get back to real heat production.

"Breakfast. Can't do much worthwhile before breakfast," Ryan said to himself.

The night had left him feeling uncertain and in danger, but the morning found him chipper, confident. At this point the adventure was a breeze: tomorrow he would backtrack to the pick-up point and find his parents. Today he wanted to build a woodland mansion. The lean-to that last night would have proved too time consuming was a perfect project for today.

The fire was roaring. Ryan took a shovelful of snow and placed it in a GI cup next to the blaze. Eating snow might quench your thirst in the short term, but in the wild it must be melted before consumed. In the long run it lowers the body core temperature too much, and if too much energy is spent warming it into a usable liquid. Hypothermia always looms large on the uneducated.

The only thing that worried Ryan was the weather. A thin ring of fog was descending and haloing the treetops. The snow was still light and dry, but seemed to be picking up in intensity. He paid it little attention though—with all weather reports agreeing before he left that there would be no storm, certainly this wasn't one to worry about. But, halos around the moon the night before have a different message for Ryan.

He turned his attention back to the shelter. He felt a unique draw to this place that had offered him survival and could conjure no reason to move from it. He had shelter from the wind, materials for building and did not require any further travel from the drop-off point miles behind him. This was *his* outcropping of trees.

The next hour found Ryan with a hatchet, disjoining the smaller spruces from their roots. By the end of the task, he had a dozen or so laid out in front of him. He began to go through the pile and strip the branches from the trunks. The difficulty that he ran into was that the trees would turn with each cut from the hatchet. This created a time-consuming, sometimes dangerous process. The downward strokes of the hatchet came close to hitting him a couple of times.

"Getting cut by my own hatchet is the last thing I need."

After the first dozen were cleared, he turned his attention to other stunted trees and saplings, knowing that he would need another couple dozen trees to make his shelter. This time he decided to strip the limbs off of each before dislodging the trunk. This made the job go much more quickly and efficiently.

In the end he had around forty sapling trunks. They ranged in size from six feet tall on down.

The next task was to find two trees of the right characteristics. He wanted two strong ones—thick, and standing about six feet apart. He carried with him the sturdiest trunks—one just taller than his own height—and two rolls of parachute cord 50 feet in length.

Ryan spotted two trees inside the grove that would serve his purpose perfectly. He walked through the small stand of woods toward them. About midway through he noticed a set of tracks that traversed the length in front of him. He bent near it and inspected it closely.

He said to himself," it's a small wolf, or a large fox."

He looked up in the sky. The spot was entirely unsheltered from the snow. Enough hadn't fallen to cover up any tracks, so he could not be sure whether it was fresh or not.

"Better keep my eyes open," he thought.

Not that he was too worried. He would be a fool to think that he could go out in the wild and not have a chance to encounter any of the animals out here. They had been living in the wilderness a long time. "Ryan, focus!!" he said to himself. First things first.

The long piece of wood served as a cross bar when he had finished securing it into place. Viewing it from the front, the initial frame of his lean-to shelter resembled a high school football goal post. The trees he found formed the base and uprights; the one he tied at four feet high across them was the crossbar. The next step was to secure the two diagonal pieces. The tip of each connected where the upright and crossbar intersected, then ran parallel to each other until the other ends rested on the ground some four feet behind the goalpost. He then took all the similarly long trunks and lined them up in the same fashion until the roof of the structure was completed.

"Now for some walls," he said.

He ordered the remaining trunks in descending order by height and separated every other one into a pile. The tallest of these he stood next to the original upright and along the diagonal roof beam. He tied it in, then put the next tallest up in the same fashion. He continued on in this way until he reached the back of the structure, where the diagonal pieces met the ground, and had completed his walls on both sides. In the end it resembled an A-frame house cut in half perfectly down the center of the roof.

"Insulation and wind protection," he said as he spread the spruce boughs over the roof and sides of his structure. He started at the bottom and worked his way to the top. That way the overlap was facing toward the lower end of his structure. Otherwise, if it rained, the water would seep through every spot where a new layer started. Not that he was worried about the rain, just about doing things right.

The remaining few branches and boughs Ryan spread along the floor of the shelter. An eight inch thick spread supplied the last insulation he would need: between him and heat sucking snow.

He sat back and admired his new home—even if it would only be his for a night. He felt a bit bad cutting down the trees, but spruce can grow almost two feet a year, so he knew they would be replenished in a relatively short time.

The only thing left to do was to transplant the fire. A lean-to is a fine structure, but with the one side completely open, is liable to let quite a bit of weather in and heat out. The wind would not be able to blow in since the shelter was located in the middle of the trees, and a fire placed a few feet in front of the shelter does the work of keeping the whole thing heated—provided it's far enough away to not start the shelter on fire.

By the time he sat beneath the lean-to, his beaming pride was only matched by his hunger. It had taken several hours to construct, but it was a fairly decent little shelter. There was a bag of stew he was saving for tonight—kind of a feast before he went back in the morning. He ate, and then crawled into the sleeping bag for the second night of sleep. The fire continued, even through the snow that was starting to pick up. He smiled proudly when he noticed that none of it fell into the shelter.

Indeed, the shelter was well-built enough to keep out the snow. But, as Ryan slept, the clouds over his head continued to drop more and more snow. In all, six to eight inches would fall before he would wake up in the morning. He was safe from the snow in the shelter. But little did Ryan know that outside the snow was changing the landscape in unrecognizable, treacherous ways.

CHAPTER VI

"Without wilderness, we will eventually lose the capacity to understand America."

Harvey Broome
(Co-founder of The Wilderness Society)

Sleep that night was comingled with a dream. Ryan awoke sporadically to feed more wood onto the fire, but would always return to the same dream. In it, he was hiking with his father. It was through high mountains that afforded a view of a valley stream below at every turn. In the dream, Ryan saw it as the most beautiful sight he had ever taken in. But whenever he would turn to his father to see the man's reaction, his father was always curiously looking behind him where he had just come on the trail.

The morning broke cold and gray. It was snowing, despite forecasts to the contrary. Ryan roused himself from the sleeping bag and shuffled out into the fresh snow. He jumped up and down next to the fire after throwing more wood on and felt the heat radiate inside and out. It would be a test to stay warm today. He wasn't going anywhere.

"If it's snowing hard enough on the day of the pickup, I'm not going to worry if you're not there," Bill had said as he dropped Ryan off. "It's too easy to get disoriented in it. Just don't travel."

Ryan knew this qualified as "hard enough."

Just beyond the camp Ryan noticed a dotted trail of imperfection on the otherwise perfect surface of snow. Wolf tracks! He stepped out to where they completely encircled his camp at a distance. Had he just not seen them yesterday? He knew that was impossible. With how hard it was snowing, there was no way that the tracks would still be there, and it was even less likely that he just hadn't noticed them. In fact his own tracks were no longer there leading up to the lean-to.

Ryan was suddenly filled with dread and anxiety.

"No. No. Oh, please, no," he repeated aloud as he rushed to the edge of the grove of trees. He walked around it a couple times and fell on his knees, looking out to the horizon.

"No, no, no . . ." He felt tears well up in his eyes. His mittened fingers were squeezing at his wool cap and hair in fear, frustration.

He was at least disoriented or worse: lost.

Without the threat of snow looming two days ago Ryan hadn't even checked what direction he had started off in. He knew he was generally travelling west, but beyond that? Ryan had no idea. He could head generally east, that was easy enough. But to find the exact pickup location? Nearly impossible. He moved swiftly across the land two days ago in his excitement—potentially putting over ten miles between himself and the starting point. A compass has 360 degrees. That would be like having a clock around him with three-hundred and sixty-minutes — and only one of them lead back to the right spot. If he was off course in walking back by even ten degrees he could potentially stray over two miles off course. And that was only *if* he could walk in a straight line.

Why had he been so reliant on footprints in the snow? Now he realized what his dream had been about. His dad always told him that when you're out walking in the wilderness, keeping direction is often as easy as just turning around. Certainly the ground might look different with snow, but particular aspects always remain—certain trees, an oddly shaped boulder. By not looking back, Ryan had given himself nothing, absolutely no way of ever retracing his path. For all he knew he could end up walking out of the trees right onto the sheet of ice from the first day—and it could be the right direction!

He paced furiously back to the shelter. Ryan was somewhere between rage at himself for stupidly getting into so many dangerous situations and fear of never getting home. When he crossed over the wolf tracks his fear began to wax. He peered at the tracks closely. They were various sizes. They had passed so close, they had circled his camp in fact, and he hadn't even heard them. It was almost a sense of violation—something had been watching him from many different angles, probably even while he slept.

The reserve of wood had gotten low since he quit replenishing it with plans to leave today. He haphazardly dumped the remaining logs on the fire to get it big. Then he slung the .22 caliber rifle around his shoulder and ventured out to get more. The easy, dry and dead wood was getting scarce. He would need to cut down a tree and let it dry if he was going to be here more than another day. His dad taught him how to build a drying kiln for wet or fresh wood in order for it to burn better.

Another day out here! Ryan let out a frustrated little roar.

The fallen tree that he had utilized on the first day to make a fire was just in front of him. He felt like something was watching him as he pulled it into pieces. A few times he snapped around to look into the trees, or out across the landscape. He piled the fragments in his arms and almost ran back to the shelter in a terror.

The fire was almost dead. The last barrage of fuel that Ryan had assaulted it with weren't catching—in fact, they were smothering it.

What would he do if the fire went out? He dropped the wood and rushed over to it. He snatched out the pieces of wood, intent on renewing the blaze.

Suddenly he felt a burning in his hand. He looked down. He must have picked up an ember on accident. His glove was slowly seething, the woolen tips glowed bright red. He plunged his hand into the snow to stop the burning. When he pulled it back out he could see through to his hand. It wasn't a large hole, but out here it could prove to be a fatal chink in his armor.

"Alright," he said looking at his hand. "Alright, just calm down. Panicking isn't going to solve anything."

The skin wasn't burned, luckily. Nothing required medical attention. *He was OK. Right now, this minute, he was OK.*

"Now, what do I need to be OK in the next minute, too?"

He carefully reassembled the wood and got the fire going. Good.

"Next . . ."

Ryan formed a new pile of wood. It was enough for at least a day.

"They're going to start looking for me—hopefully by tomorrow."

He knew this was more than just a bit hopeful. His dad wouldn't expect him back today, and if it was still snowing tomorrow he just *might* go looking. Within two days, for sure, though. Their neighbor, Mac Stewart, had a small plane with skis. Bill would probably ask him to help fly the area to search for Ryan. But with so many directions that Ryan could have taken off in, how would they find him?

There was almost no wind, but the snow kept falling. Could the storm be in a stall? Could it just be sitting overhead, dropping now until it died? People who have lived in Alaska long enough all remember a time that storms did this and dropped so much snow that only the roofs of cabins were visible—and some of those caved in from the weight.

The snow and fog wouldn't last forever. All he had to do was survive until they were gone and make himself noticeable to a plane. At least the panicking was behind him. As long as he was OK during the moment he was in and planning how to be OK in the next one, everything would be fine.

He closed his eyes and felt some of his worry lessen. The wolves were probably around him again tonight. But they wouldn't come near the fire. And if they did? Well, he made sure the .22 and his knife were nearby, just in case.

CHAPTER VII

*"Is not the sky a father and the earth the mother, and
are not all living things with feet or wings, of
roots their children?"*

Black Elk (Medicine Man of the Lakota Sioux)

Ryan allowed himself to wake slowly. He had slept long and hard and now he had a disoriented feeling. What was dream? What was real? For a moment he thought about the wolves with the same relief that one remembers a bad dream—away and safe from a terror in the night. He pushed himself up and remembered that he *was* lost, that there *were* wolf prints around his shelter last night. Rather than waking from a nightmare, he had awoken back into one.

And to make matters worse, the sky had fallen twice last night. First, it was obvious the snow had continued to dump. His fuel reserves were now a heap of debris beneath four or five inches of smooth white. Second, the clouds had descended and made a fog so thick and murky that Ryan could not even see to the perimeter of his small circle of trees.

Not only was he snowed in, he was also hidden.

He tried hard to think about whether it mattered that he was hidden or not. What day number was he on in the woods? Those concerns of time and amount of days have a tendency to slip away in the wilderness. With no itinerary, appointments to keep, dates or anniversaries to remember the mind does not naturally count the days. The mind becomes concerned with survival, the next move, to live through today before worrying about tomorrow. If this was his fourth day it did not matter that he was hidden because nobody would be looking for him yet. If it was the fifth day, they might be searching. It definitely didn't feel as though it had been six days, and probably not five.

An orientation regarding what day it was and how many it had been was important, Ryan knew. His dad had told him that a trait people share who survive experiences of being lost in the woods is that they maintain a log of days, even a journal if possible. He had nothing to write with or on. What other way is there to track days? He looked around the camp and noticed the smooth trunk of a sapling. He got out his knife and decided to cut a grove into the sapling for each day he was in the wilderness. It would be a crude demarcation of days, but it was better than nothing.

Now that the system was in place he had only to remember the days. First day, he was traveling and fell through the ice. That was an easy one. He must have built the snow trench that night. One cut in the tree. Ok, second day. Second day, he built the shelter. Good. That was the day he was still planning to come home. Did it snow that day? No, it was that night. Two cuts in the tree. Third day, he realized his tracks were gone. That was an easy one, too. But what about finding out the wolf prints were around? That was yesterday, but was that the same day as when he found his tracks were gone? They were both huge events and seemed worthy of taking up their own days, but as he closed his eyes and thought through the sequence of events, he realized that they both happened on the same day. Three cuts in the tree. And, today. Four cuts.

"From now on," he thought to himself, "first thing every morning, I will put a cut in the tree." It wouldn't do to not remember at the end of the day whether he had put in the cut or not, and even with just three days there it was almost impossible to go back and disentangle the different days. A system would only work if it wasn't too confusing—especially out here.

So, it was the fourth day. Not too bad. It made him worry less about the fog. No one would be looking for him, anyway. Plus, even if they had thought to look for him they probably wouldn't have the plane out. There wouldn't be any sense in it. The important thing was to get ready for tomorrow when hopefully the fog would lift and they would be looking for him.

Ryan knew how big Alaska was. He had a rough idea of the size of the wilderness area. But it wasn't until he thought about someone trying to find him in all of it that he realized how big it was. He was this tiny thing on the face of the snow somewhere. And his dad—even with his barrel-chest and powerful arms—was another small thing on the face of the snow somewhere else. What chance did two specks have of running into each other?

The trick to signal making, he had learned, was to make yourself bigger than you are. That was primary. And, secondary, you had to know the code. Being bigger than you are isn't that difficult. All he had to do was find a way to contrast the snow so that someone looking out of a plane would notice the difference. The best he could do for now was the evergreen branches. He started pulling the largest of them from towards a clearing. He found himself surprisingly timid about stepping away from the trees. He knew the frozen ice was nearby, and doubted that he could save himself from such an ordeal again. Even though he scanned the ground and saw stumps and the outline of swells of ground in front of him, he still stepped gingerly away from the trees to lay the first branch on the ground. A dozen trips later he was more certain and began to form out the big V that his dad had taught him meant that someone needed help. There were enough pilots zig zagging the Alaskan airspace that maybe someone would see him, even if it wasn't his dad.

By time he was done, each leg of the V was about thirty feet long and two or three feet across. He would have preferred it to be fifty feet long and six feet across, but there just weren't enough branches around to make it happen.

Ryan was beginning to wonder if the fog would lift. He sat next to the fire and watched the world around him. Everything was slow, there was nothing to do. He decided to crawl into his shelter, into his sleeping bag, and take a nap to pass the day. He briefly thought of his original objective: Learn about himrself and learn the lesson that the wilderness has to teach and celebrate the rite of passage from boyhood to manhood. But other things had occupied his mind.

He imagined thermometers plunging all around him. When he opened his eyes it was noticeably colder than it had been before. He was safe, there was fire and he was bundled up well, but there was something daunting about the air around him.

And it was getting dark. He slipped out of the bag and into the air and pushed more wood onto the fire. He scanned around and couldn't see the signal. He stepped to the edge of the camp where he had built it and realized why. He also realized why everything felt so cold. It wasn't a terribly major one, but there had been an ice storm while he slept. Bits of frozen rain had collected on everything. The branches were beautiful. Crystals of ice had formed around each individual branch, twig and needle. It almost seemed that the trees had turned into opaque, frosted glass. While the branches were beautiful, they were also completely worthless as a signaling device. He would have to scrape the ice off the branches tomorrow. It was too cold and dark to worry about it now, plus he was too hungry.

Ryan probably had not drunk hot chocolate in more than three years and he almost never ate fast food. But, for some reason his mind was on a steaming cup of syrupy chocolate with marshmallows melting over the top and a greasy bag of salty fries and a huge burger.

He stopped and closed his eyes to force the vision out. That wasn't going to help anything. He couldn't start thinking about what he didn't—

There was a thrashing coming from his outcropping of trees. Something, somewhere. His eyes were open and trying to adjust and focus into the dusken night. He couldn't make out any shapes or hear any other noises. His mind was on the wolves, but also on his father. Either one could be looking for him. Ryan generally figured in he heard something in the wilderness that it was a bird, or some other harmless animal. Predators you usually don't hear. A predator that makes noises while stalking would probably have died of starvation long ago. But out here, he didn't let that thinking go too far. The wolves could have been searching around, smelling in the waning light. But what if it was his dad?

"Make another noise," he whispered to himself.

But nothing came.

And now he second guessed himself. Maybe it had been farther off. Maybe it was a sound that had come from over the hills and across the fast slopes of snow. What if someone was looking for him?

"I'm over here!" he shouted. "Hey! Hey! Over here!"

The cold and snow and fog absorbed his voice. There was a defeated lack of reverberation to sounds out here. And after his voice was gone, there were no other sounds. Somewhere he had hoped he would hear a response. But a larger part of him he had been ignoring knew that no one was there.

Maybe it was just a tree cracking under the weight of the ice and snow. It did happen. He hoped it was a tree. But a larger part of him that he was trying to ignore knew that it wasn't.

CHAPTER VIII

"The survival of the human species is inescapably linked with the survival of all other forms of life."

Michael Frome
(American outdoor and environmental writer)

As he unslung the .22 he noticed that the barrel was full of ice. He must have dropped it somewhere along the way, or pushed with it in his race from the ice. Either way, it now had ice caked inside of it and the bolt action was cemented in place. As anything other than a bludgeon it was useless to him now, and as there was no safe way to warm it, it would remain that way until he got home.

And for once, he noticed, the thought of home passed by without any lingering. He suddenly felt wild: eyes taken over by instinct bouncing at all points in the immediate area. Something was here. He could feel it.

The rifle fell uselessly to the ground. The only protection left was the hatchet that Ryan unhooked from his belt. Minutes passed with him frozen in that same spot. All of his senses were engaged to locate anything that moved and to decipher where it was.

As if on a cue, the earth suddenly lightened all around him. For a moment he honestly believed that his vigilance had triggered some sort of vestigial night vision section of his brain, but when he looked above him he saw the fog and clouds had begun to part out. The moon was shining down.

The storm was breaking.

He took advantage of the reflected light, the light that seemed to originate from both the moon above and snow below, though it just reflected off of each. The fog was lifting all around and allowed the corners of perception to lengthen, illuminate, reveal their secrets. From what he saw, they had none.

What did survival entail? Sitting here, panicking with every day that passed? By the time anyone found him he would likely have gone feral, scurrying up trees to avoid every sound. His mind might be so damaged from the constant stress that he would make some hasty decision that would take him right off a cliff.

"Stay where you are," he thought to himself. It's what he was always told—it makes the job of finding you easier.

But there were the wolf prints. That was certain. They were around here, somewhere. Certainly there were other things to run into out in the wild, but not many of them could be much more dangerous than what was already there. And there was no telling when they would look for him, or where. No, the best idea was to engage his mind and actions in getting home.

But for now he needed sleep. The trip through the snow would not be easy by any means. Even if he happened back the exact route from which he had arrived, it would be longer, more arduous hours with the additional snow and mounting fatigue. A good sleep would work wonders in the long run.

Ryan enveloped himself in his sleeping bag. He filled it with every piece of wool clothing he had to maintain warmth. His bed of boughs kept him above the frozen ground, and he pulled his stocking cap over his entire face. His mind kept replaying what actions he might take tomorrow . . .

Something startled him awake. He had not even realized that he fell asleep. He was not even sure if he had. But something brought him back to full, instant awareness. Ryan ripped the cap off his face and scrambled to peer out of his enclosure. The fire was an ashed-over char heap. Something had roused him. Something set off an alarm that his subconscious refused to ignore.

Something moved. In the distance. A quiet, bouncing gait. There was no confusing what he saw with a hallucination. No faulty perception produced lines so fine. His heart began to rush blood into his ears, his head felt woozy from the surplus being pumped. Adrenaline was racing to every appendage and corner of his young body. Something out there was a danger to him.

Something else moved, in the shadow of a tree.

A pathetic panic flushed his body. There was no fight or flight response, because he was in the only thing to which he could fly—and even there, safety did not prevail. There was no fight or flight, because without his rifle—and perhaps even with it—he was no match for something that would be stalking him out here.

Then three, four figures emerged. The dim specters moved on four legs and Ryan's vision was acute enough that even from thirty feet he could see hackling backlit by the iridescent snow. Their heads were leading below the bodies, snouts near the ground. Their movements and parts were fluid, timed as though to a chronometer.

Ryan cursed and pushed himself to standing. He threw his arms in the air with his sleeping bag bunched high above his head and let out a primal scream that even frightened him. In the next second he knew the beasts would have a fight or flight of their own. He was hoping that the violent noise and smokescreen size he was putting up would be enough to spook whatever they were.

Ryan discharged four full lungs of air. His body shook hotly and his head became light. So much blood was sweeping through his head that his vision blurred over. He had no idea if the animals had stopped, run away or continued advancing. He bent to the stack of wood and began to pile it atop the fire pit. His hands gripped the pieces to find the thinnest branches that would catch the quickest from the diminishing embers. Still unbalanced from the exertion of screaming, Ryan bent down and blew his hardest on the embers and quickly felt the heat rising to his face.

"Burn," he urged in a low, desperate voice he didn't recognize. *"Burn!"*

When he rose to his feet it was with his hatchet in hand. He stripped his gloves off to feel the nicks and imperfections of the old wooden handle across his palm and fingers. Even with sweaty hands, the hatchet was less likely to get pulled away from him without the gloves than with them. Though the gloves might provide some protection, if he lost the hatchet he would be beyond the need for any padding anyway.

The rising fire made the outer rim of the camp darken. Ryan could no longer make out the shapes that he knew were there just moments ago.

"Are they gone?" he thought to himself. "Did I scare them off?"

His long underwear was stretched along his back and was stuck to his skin. In his panic he had sweated through them and now they pulled the heat from his body rather than insulating as they should have.

The cold, fear and adrenaline all combined to rattle his body with tremors. Ryan unclenched his teeth and allowed himself to drop to a crouch beside the fire. He stared into it, trying to replay the images in his mind for some other clue as to what was out there.

A moment later a chill raked through his body. He sensed *something* around him. It felt everywhere. The adrenaline had almost all surged away, and he was left with a heartbeat that seemed to be sending huge waves of blood through his system.

Ryan slowly rose and turned around a degree at a time. By the time he was facing the small, glassy reflections of light, he was standing between them and the fire. Two, three, five sets of eyes began to emerge out of the darkness around him. As though realizing it had been spotted, one of the creatures let out a sound that was a mix between a huffing sigh and a growl. It stepped forward into the lights' reach, and the others followed suit.

MacKenzie Valley wolves (canis lupus occidentalis). From ground to shoulder they stood three feet high. Each frame carried one hundred pounds, easy. For food, they would travel seventy miles in a day. For food, they would bring down and devour a full grown moose.

Ryan pivoted backwards, almost falling behind the fire. He wanted the heat, the light, the roar of his creation to stand between him and the wolves.

All five canines, now in full view, spread throughout the camp around him. Was it his smell? The moose jerky? By what had they been drawn?

The wolves regarded him again with their intelligent, defiant eyes. Ryan thought to make a run for it, but where? Into the shelter? Not much of a shelter for keeping wolves out. Out into the wilderness? That would just serve to cloak his attackers.

The alpha wolf of the group stood face to face with Ryan on the other side of the fire, which licked up above Ryan's head by now. The eyes penetrated through the fire and were locked on Ryan's. Ryan thought to look away, not wanting to unintentionally challenge the animal, but he also didn't want to signal submission. More than either of those, he continued looking without having made a decision about it.

Then the large alpha growled for a moment. The next a growl came from behind him, then to the side, then all the wolves were growling. Once again he saw the hackles rise in a long line down the backbones of the animals. They stood tense, unmoving, but emitting a simmering growl that seemed ready to boil over into boldfaced aggression at any moment.

For no reason, Ryan began to pile more wood on the fire. Instead of the tight tepee formation in which wood is usually stacked, though, he let the bottoms of the pieces splay out in such a way that made the fire grow wide as well as high. One of the branches he picked up had long graying fingers to which dry, dead needles clung. This piece was nearly as tall as he was and he dipped the bristle end of it into the fire. It caught quickly and the flames spread to each province of the branch. Ryan held the crackling flame high and heavy above his head.

"What are we going to do?" he asked aloud. "What are we here for?" Ryan began speaking whatever words came into his mind. It was not planned, but as he heard the words come out he realized that they sounded a lot tougher than what he might usually think to say.

"Are we here to fight? Are we here to live? Maybe there's no difference for you, but for me there is."

He began to wave the towering branch from side to side. Bits of ember dropped all around him and landed on the ground before disappearing. The fire left streaks of light in its path back and forth through the sky. It was like a shooting star that kept retracing its arcing path through the night.

"I'm lost out here," he said aloud, in rhythm with the swaying branch. "I fell through ice the other morning, and pulled myself out. I am lucky to be alive."

He continued on with his story, about making the shelter and losing his footprints. After he had been talking he realized that the wolves were no longer in an aggressive posture. The coldness in their eyes had been replaced with a curiosity. They gazed for a few moments at the sweeping fire in the air, then back again at the human speaking to them. They seemed almost mesmerized by each.

Then, during a pause in the story, the alpha wolf blew a mist of air through his nose. The water vapor hitting the cold air hung like smoke in a still room. The wolf then turned and walked back into the woods. Silently, the others followed.

Ryan fell to his knees. Physically he had yet to recover from falling through the ice. This night, however long it had lasted, had drained the last of his energy. Though he had never felt the mental toughness that he felt right now, he cried out of a physical weakness. The emotional stress had taxed his muscles as strenuously as the shivering had days before. And now his body began to shiver as well. He had sweated through his clothes and knew that if he left them on and went to bed—as his body was pleading with him to do—they would freeze and sap even more energy.

Luckily the fire was looming large as a bonfire. Ryan was able to peel his clothes off without the freeze affecting him. He hung his clothes on branches near the fire and watched as they steamed into the night.

In fifteen minutes they were dry. He knew it was the right thing as he lay down in clothes that were—at least for the moment—as warm as if they had just come from a dryer. But he had little time to think about this as he collapsed into sleep.

CHAPTER IX

"Two roads diverged in a woods, and I—I took the one less traveled by, And that has made all the difference."

Robert Frost
(American Poet) The Road Less Traveled

The sleep rejuvenated him as much as it could, which, while still quite a bit, was not sufficient tonic for his depleted energy reserves or fatigued muscles. In fact, through his entire body lay a constant soreness and ache.

Ryan also woke already reserved to the notion of moving on. The day was clear and beginning to brighten, so there was little to cause him to deviate from the plan he had set in motion last night. One glance at the size and frequency of the wolf tracks circling the camp were enough to solidify in his mind that it was time to move on.

But first he had developed a system that required his fidelity. He unfolded the blade of his small knife and recorded the day. Five cuts in the tree.

"It's too bad that there's no way to record what happened those days," Ryan said, looking at the simple marks on the tree. "These don't show what I went through or had to do to survive."

But Ryan also knew that he wasn't recording what happened, he was remembering the days, trying to survive.

His first order of business before leaving was to uncover and rearrange the signal. A V would do no good, but an arrow could indicate in which direction he left. Ryan oriented himself with the sun. When he left he had traveled west, so now he should travel back east in hopes of making it home.

Knocking the ice from the branches was proving to be a difficult chore. A few minutes into the task Ryan decided to see if he could make things any easier. He brought his lantern near the fire and dabbed some of the oil onto the end of a branch. He needed to conserve as much of the oil as possible, but this was a worthy use of it as well. The lantern itself could ignite if it was left too close to the fire, so Ryan hung it high above and away from the flames.

He put the oil slicked end of the branch in the fire and watched it begin to burn. The fire at the end only burned the oil though, and just blackened the branch end beneath. This rudimentary torch he brought down and used to melt the ice from the signal. With the branches uncovered, he rearranged the V into an arrow pointing toward the horizon in which the sun had risen. Though there are sometimes just a few degrees difference between the spot in the sky in which the sun rises and sets in Alaska, the main idea was to give a plane an idea of which way he had set off. The rest of the morning Ryan spent rearranging the branches and packing his supplies.

The handkerchief wrapped provisions were beginning to dwindle. Three days worth of food was now being stretched into a fifth day. In this barren wilderness, getting more was beyond any question—at least without the rifle. Ryan bit off two small chunks of the jerky and chewed it slowly, savoring every second of it. It was probably all the food that he would eat today.

He was suddenly struck by the image of his mother standing in their kitchen. For all he knew it was exactly what she was doing. In his mind she was looking out the window with an untouched cup of cold coffee sitting next to her. They had to assume that he was lost, and with that prospect looming over her, she would probably have difficulty completing even perfunctory tasks. At least his dad would have tasks to execute in arranging a search flight and trying to find him. For all Ryan knew, his dad could be buckling into the seat right now and getting ready for take-off. But his mom was stuck on the ground, forced to wait for someone else to give her the news—news that, hopefully, would come. The only thing worse would be if they went into the second or third week of not—

"Stop," he said aloud. "Stop thinking about this."

He stood up quickly and started pacing back and forth in front of his packed supplies.

"Stupid, so *stupid*. Why didn't you look where you were going? Why didn't you do what you were supposed to. You're *stupid!*"

He could feel that he was starting to lose his focus. He pushed all thoughts out of his mind. The teachings of survival were the primary things to remember; past mistakes and what his mother and father might be doing needed to fall prey to a bad memory. Forgetting mistakes but not lessons learned, that was the key to survival here. Maybe that was the key to survival anywhere.

With that thought the driving force in his mind, Ryan stood beneath the weight of his supplies and pushed his arm toward the east with all fingers extended.

"East!" he exclaimed.

The snow crunched beneath his snowshoes. The first steps out were the hardest. But Ryan knew that he would be walking for several hours until he either found the drop-off point or where he would stop for the night. The whole way he would stay near the trees and other signs of solid ground. He would take no shortcuts. He would stay vigilant and focused. He would survive.

CHAPTER X

"Not to have known—as most men have not—either the mountain or the desert is not to have known one's self."

Joseph Wood Krutch
(American writer, naturalist)

Ryan's shadow was beginning to stretch along the ground. There was a feeling somewhere inside of him that he had failed to cover as much ground as what his walking would suggest. His unwillingness to risk another water fall through had forced him to circumnavigate around the snowy valleys that might hide a spring beneath. At no time had he seen something that he recognized, nor any tell-tale sign or sound of another person. In fact, the quiet, slow monotony of the march had lulled him into a hypnotic saunter. His legs didn't burn unless he thought about them, and the hunger had been so constant since the day began that he had become either numb to it or accustomed.

The shadow lengthening was an alarm though. Ryan was sure that he would stumble over the top of a hill and suddenly see his goal, or someone out looking for him. Each time the horizon extended with no hint of recognition was a small defeat. Now he had to decide to stop, to let go of the desire to be out of the wilderness tonight. Going much later without a campsite picked out would be treacherous.

He scanned the treed area for a suitable spot. Just ahead he noticed that there was a spine of rocks lifting into the air like the curve of a surfacing whale. If it was a ridge he might be able to see the land all around unimpeded. Ryan silently estimated that it was another twenty minutes of hiking, and that this corner of the earth would be nearly enveloped by dusk by time he reached the top. It was worth the extra time and risk, though, so Ryan went for it.

The top did afford the view he expected it would, but not the one he hoped for. All around, for miles, there was nothing familiar or human. It was such a humiliating defeat that he didn't even yell out from the top as he had planned. Dejectedly, Ryan slouched back down the other side of the hill. There was no sense in going down the same we he'd come up. Plus, the eastern slope would likely shield him from the wind that would pick up during the night.

This side of the outcropping jutted out into a little shelf over the earth, creating a dry crevice of rock just at ground level. This formation was really the best thing that he could hope for: he and all of his belongings would be out of the elements, and he could build a fire just in front of where he would sleep that would radiate into and warm the rocks while he slept. He would have to make another bed of spruce boughs, but that would be simple enough.

Ryan set out into the trees and began collecting dead wood. He was on his third trip of gathering, returning and stacking when he noticed a pair of tracks. Snowshoes! They were less than two hundred yards away from the outcropping where he was camping. Someone had walked by just east of the outcropping, and Ryan himself had just an hour earlier arrived from the west.

"Hey!" he shouted. "Hey!"

He waited, but heard nothing.

Ryan leaned back, cupped his hands over his mouth, and yelled, "Anyone heeere? Heeey! I'm heeeere!"

Nothing responded.

He trudged over to the tracks while still shouting, "Hey, hey, hey! Here! Here! Here!"

When he was above them he inspected the print. His dad's snowshoe left a mark that was longer, narrower than his own. He stepped in sideways to the path and found a left foot print. He slowly lowered his own snowshoe into it. The impression cast by the footstep curled, curved and dimpled in the exact spots as his own.

Ryan exhaled and dropped his head, arms and shoulders. A second defeat of the day. A huge defeat. While it wasn't literally impossible for someone to be out looking for him with the exact same snowshoe design, it was unlikely. It was his footprint. He had left those marks.

The outcropping was small enough that Ryan was able to run halfway around it in less than five minutes. On the other side he saw the footprints where he had approached the outcropping and climbed it. He ran the other half circle around the outcropping and came across the straight line he had laid earlier in the day. He had passed this point earlier, sometime in the day. Ryan turned and followed those steps in reverse back to where he had decided to camp.

He was lost. There were no questions. So lost that he didn't even know how to get away from where he was. Who knows how many loops he had walked in that day? Was he even as far from where he had started as what he thought? He was walking in circles the whole time. Many times the terrain causes people who are lost to do that.

"No self pity," he said to himself in a low, certain voice. "No room for it out here. At least not for it and survival."

He had a bed beneath the rocks and enough wood to set on fire through the whole night if he wanted to. Aside from being hungry, lost and tired, nothing was wrong.

Ryan scraped the snow with the butt of the rifle to reveal a small patch of earth. He put the petroleum jelly-laden cotton balls and toilet paper on the ground and piled small bits of kindling and tinder above them. He reached into his bag and scrounged for the flint and steel. He found the steel easily, but the other end of the rawhide string that should have been tying it to the flint hung empty.

The light was slipping away. The last bits of yellow were being snuffed out in the western sky by purples and dark blues of night. Ryan wouldn't even be able to light his lantern without the flint.

"No," Ryan willed aloud.

He began to pull everything out of his bag, organizing it into areas. His lantern was gone. He must have left it hanging from the tree at the last camp.

"No," he said again.

He shook his fists for a moment to resist the urge to yell at himself for being so stupid again, and pounding his fists into his thighs. None of these things would accomplish anything.

Ryan began going through each individual pack. He had supplies that he hadn't even opened yet. Not food, implements. He silently hoped he would make it through the night to use them tomorrow. Maybe there was a packet of matches, or a lighter somewhere. But each packet only contained a wrapping, or iodine tablets, or gauze pads or a swiss army knife, or a magnifying glass. Though not a thing to create fire.

In a final act of desperation, Ryan plunged his hand into the empty bag and let his fingers scurry along the corners and crevices like a mouse hugging close to a wall.

Then his fingers ran into something. A leather flap at the bottom of the bag had an object wedged beneath. The flint.

This feeling of life was coming in thin slices.

Ryan pulled the flint out and squeezed it tightly in his hands for a moment. He would have fire, companionship and survival for at least one more night.

CHAPTER XI

For sleeping on essentially a pile of rocks, Ryan found himself the most comfortable that night that he had been since his whole journey began. The rocks surrounding him absorbed and emanated the heat from the fire, the result of which was Ryan feeling warmth from two hundred and seventy degrees around him. When the first light of day came into the crystal night he woke with it. He was refreshed and content.

In fact, if the area wasn't a dense forest surrounded in high trees, he would have thought to stay there. But, as it was, there was no hope of anyone finding him in there. It was impossible to send a signal visible from above.

The compass has a red and white needle pinned in a clear plastic case. The numbers around the circular metal casing turn to allow for different degree readings. If that was a question on Jeopardy, Ryan would get it right, despite not really knowing what it was for. He held the device in his fingers and stared down at it. The red end of the arrow pointed toward magnetic north which Ryan knew—because of how far north he was in Alaska—was not really north at all. Anyway, without a map it was useless to use it for finding anything. The only thing it might help with is in keeping himself from walking in circles. He would determine which direction to walk, read the compass markings, and make sure the needle stayed pointing at the same number the whole day.

Ryan etched a mark for the new day. Six cuts in the walking stick.

For some reason the thought of bacon and eggs would not leave his mind. Ryan closed his eyes to block out the images, but even the smell of the food felt so real he almost would have thought that someone had a frying pan spitting grease nearby. It did him no good to think about food, he didn't have much left. But neither did it do good to keep himself from thinking about food, he did it nonetheless.

At full daylight Ryan decided to get a move on. The compass was on a string that he hung around his neck, to remind himself to check the direction every now and again. He kicked snow over the fire until he was satisfied it was smothered, reassembled his pack, and took off toward where the sun had risen. His footsteps marked the beat of a silent prayer he was making that he would be found that day. He would do anything to be found.

Travel was easier than it had been any of the other days. It may have been that he was growing accustomed to the lack of food on long hikes, or that his expectations had sharply decreased and he was resigned to walking an entire day so long as he was making distance at a generally good pace. He knew that he didn't know where he was going, but that didn't change the fact that the snow wasn't so fresh anymore—that it had packed down and no longer allowed even the snowshoes to sink down with every step. It was firm, solid footing, and he progressed across the terrain rapidly through the day.

Ryan was thankful for the compass, especially in the deep forest in which he seemed to be engulfed. Even just the act of stepping around a tree could have thrown off his trajectory. Every few minutes he rechecked the compass to make sure that he was at least heading in a straight line.

A large rock formation sat with all the force gravity allowed it ahead. Through the years, wind and water had eroded one side of it to resemble the back and seat of a large, prehistoric chair. He had been going for a few hours and decided it was a good time for a rest.

It was only then, after the sounds of crunching snow and dismounting of his pack had died in the woods, that he heard another noise. It was a long noise, far away. It was a constant drone, like a mosquito the size of a fist would make. But it was also mechanical, synthetic, like the humming of electricity through power lines.

Ryan stood up at attention. Looking around. Then he realized that the sound was gone. He kept thinking that maybe it was there, then he would listen hard and wonder if he even really heard anything in the first place. He stood in place, confused, trying not to make a noise that would cover up whatever might be out there. After five minutes the droning started again. It sounded like a loud vacuum cleaner through an open window three houses away—a steady humming.

It was a plane. His dad. Mac. They were coming for him!

He turned in the direction from which the noise hummed. Tall timber passed around his left and right and he dashed through atop his snowshoes. The plane was nowhere in sight, but neither was anything else in the sky—which meant that nothing up there would be able to see him either. It was an impossible thing for Ryan to make himself larger than a forest on such short notice. He needed to find a break in the trees, a wide opening, and hope that the plane happened to be flying over and looking down at that exact moment.

"Here! Here!" he shouted through heaps of breath as the sound of the engine grew more and more faint. Finally, after the sound had receded completely, he stopped. "Here," he said softly, not wanting to overpower any fragile chance of hearing the plane again.

Disappointment and hopelessness swept over him, crushing down on him with a force that his legs couldn't carry. Ryan crumpled to the ground and was weeping, murmuring, "Turn back, please come back, look for me, turn back . . ."

He kept speaking the words as though a mantra until he realized his throat and jaw hurt. Suddenly he was too sad to cry. He lay there for an even longer time feeling the self-pity pool around him, knowing he was going to die out there in the wilderness, so it might as well be right there. Why waste more time? Why build more fire? The wilderness around him might as well be infinite.

Suddenly everything that he had been through seemed a waste. It would have been so much easier had he just let himself slip under the ice on that first day. Everything since then had been cruel prolongations, delays of the inevitable.

For the first time since he had been out there, Ryan knew that that wilderness was where he would die.

CHAPTER XII

For the next couple of hours, Ryan's mind replayed the events since he had lost his way. Each step was like reliving a regret and he was just as hard on himself as anyone who finds himself in a bad situation. He cringed and closed his eyes tight against every mistake that he had made, every opportunity that he missed to remember his father's teachings.

What changed the trajectory of his emotions, however, was the thought of the arrow that he had built. Despite being lost and having walked in circles, it was likely that the plane had not flown close enough for him to hear by mistake. Probably they had been out searching and had seen the indicator of the direction and had flown that way to find him. Too bad, of course, that he had not stayed put: he would have been found already. Of course, along with that is the possibility that he would have been found as bones picked clean by the wolves. The imagination is a formidable foe when allowed to linger.

Ryan sat up. He could feel the difference between how he felt now and for the previous hours. The difference was the small successes like the arrow and shelters. With those things on his mind, he had a bit of hope. He trained his mind on those few positives—and the fact that they *were* looking for him. Ryan finally pushed himself to his feet and walked back for his pack and rifle.

"Right now Dad would be proud of me," he said aloud. His mind began replaying all the years of shelter building and fires started from flint and steel that his dad had been with him through. He thought of the three of them—himself, his dad and mom—sitting around the Texas campfires through his younger years. He thought of his mother's smile and his father's laughter. He felt the grit from his palms press against the corner of his eyes as he tried to blot the tears away.

Fear and loneliness were pushing him along a rollercoaster of emotion.

Ryan composed himself for a moment and considered what he most needed to do. Survival was the big idea, and in order to achieve it, he needed to do what he had been doing for the past few days: creating fire, finding shelter, and waiting to be found. The plane had been nearby, and he knew that they often flew a grid pattern when searching for something: a straight line, a ninety-degree turn for a half mile, then another straight line parallel to the first. He was close somewhere along that line if it was in fact what the pilot was doing. Perhaps he had just to find an opening in the forest. No forest stretches forever.

Before hoisting his burden back upon his shoulders, Ryan checked his small pouch of food reserves. All that remained was such a small, meager amount that he couldn't imagine how he could divide it into two days. After today the three-week countdown would start.

Not that it was any consolation. He felt as though the inside of his stomach was rubbing his backbone and he could feel his boniness starting to press through his parka. It seemed like the countdown without food had been going on for a couple of days.

The destination-less march commenced again. For two hours or more he continued forward, checking the compass from time to time to maintain a straight orientation, and neither seeing a break in the trees nor hearing the return of the engine.

Ryan rested himself against a tree. Wherever he stopped for the night, he would have to remember to melt some snow for drinking water. His canteen was nearly empty. He threw his head back to take in a half-mouthful and listened to the water sloshing gently inside the canteen. He stood still, and listened to the water settle against the metallic walls and his mouth. Something was wrong.

His arm slowly dropped along his side. It was perfectly silent. No wind, no sounds of open space, no animals, nothing. Ryan could hear the air he was breathing passing through his throat just behind his ears. Then came the echo of chimes through the woods. Faint, distant, but certain. Chimes? Where were the chimes coming from?

At first they were on his right, then, unmistakably, they came from behind him. Far off, but moving all around.

His dad had told him a campfire story about chimes in the wilderness. At the time, Ryan had thought it was just a lame attempt to scare him, but his dad insisted that it was true—at least that he had really been told about it.

I was fifteen and was leaving a supply shop in Tok, Alaska. I had purchased new snowshoes for the winter and had them strapped along my back.

I remember hearing windchimes and stopping to look at them just outside of the store. They were magnificent—bronze in color, with such a pure, relaxing tone.

Suddenly an old man with even older eyes was next to me. His voice would have blended in with a soft wind whispering across tall grass.

"Athabascans do not like chimes," he said. "It is what lost travelers hear before Arulataq appears."

I had heard of Athabascans before. They were the first peoples to come to the northern lands.

"What is Arulataq?" I asked him.

The corners of his mouth were pulling back and forth like he was twitching or cold. He pointed to the snowshoes on my back.

"If you hear chimes while you are out in the wilderness, it is time to move on to somewhere else."

I looked back at the chimes and turned to ask the man more about Arulataq, but he was gone.

Was this what the old man had supposedly told his father about? They were unmistakable, these sounds. They sounded of hollowed metal, but also had a sense of crackling crystal about them. They pierced through the trees.

Suddenly Ryan was overcome with fear. He looked down at his compass to get his heading. He turned to ninety degrees and sprinted away from the chimes. The compass was at the bottom frame of his view, and Ryan glanced at it every few seconds to make sure he was heading in a straight course through the trees. He realized he was counting his frantic footsteps, and somewhere in his mind the plan formulated to turn after the internal pedometer reached three hundred. When he reached the number, he turned ninety degrees again, so he was back on his original heading, and began frantically running again.

"Three hundred more," he thought to himself. "Then I'll turn another ninety degrees back, to put me on my original path. After that, I'll turn up again and will be on the same line I started."

It made perfect sense in his mind. His navigation plot on a map would look like three sides of a square, with the last side the line that he should have stayed on, but that certainly led across the path of those chimes.

Even in the canopied forest, the light seemed to drop as suddenly as if on a dimmer. Ryan was out of breath, and he could no longer keep the frenetic pace he had been. He slowed to a walk, but continued counting his steps. He consciously took larger strides to simulate running, just to be sure that he ended up in the right place. Not that there was anything better about one trajectory than another, so long as he didn't stray into circling, but Ryan felt that some sense of order, control was necessary right now.

Without explanation, Ryan's hair bristled. He could feel it standing stiff beneath his heavy parka and pack. He held stiffly silent as a shiver worked its way from his lower back, through his ribs, over his shoulders and finally into the top of his head. He didn't know how he knew, but something was following him.

He was almost back on his straight line when he spotted in the snow a disturbance. It looked as if clumsy children had trampled down a fresh snow at their bus stop. It was an unnatural chaos, especially when it broke the surrounding uniformity.

Ryan stepped close to it.

While most markings within it were disturbed by one another, every here and there Ryan recognized a spot perfect for casting a mold. They were definitely bear tracks. Contrary to popular belief, most bears don't leave behind a claw mark as part of their footprint. This one did. The long, curved nails jutted out several inches from the thick padding of the toes on the still-fresh tracks. Unfortunately, they meant only one thing.

Ryan shakily lowered the gun from his shoulder and made sure the chamber was loaded.

Not that a .22 would do anything more than mildly irritate a grizzly. Then it hit him. He had not cleaned out the barrel from ice. It was still just a club.

CHAPTER XIII

*"In God's wildness lies the hope of the world—the great
fresh, unblighted, unredeemable wilderness."*

John Muir
(American naturalist and founder of the Sierra Club)

Ryan watched the line of tracks that didn't make any sense. They
stretched through the trees a few steps, then shifted in a turn away
from the direction he was following. He lowered his head and walked
away from them warily.

Bears should have been hibernating. It was still late winter, it was cold.
But the tracks were there nonetheless. A grizzly had opened up her
den, stretched those dainty little killers at the end of her paws, thought
about her hunger, and trounced off looking for him.

The tough thing about bears—especially griz—is how strong and
relentless they are. With its mind set to doing so, the toughest of bear
can find the smallest nail hold and pull a door off a car to get to a
smell inside. They could push through the thickest scrub brush like it
was nothing more than fog. Ryan knew there was nothing around that
offered safety: even if he scrambled up a tree, a griz could easily follow,
simply push it over or wait until you tire.

Ryan knew it was probably just the worry making sounds come out of
the wilderness, but he heard what he thought was a low growl from the
bushes around him. The thought that it was just his imagination staved
off none of the fear. He started his legs in a shaky trot, but soon, with

his .22 held innocuously in his hands, the boy began running through the trees like a soldier in panicked retreat.

Alders blurred on all sides, and before he knew it he realized he was turning wildly to avoid each tree, altering direction so often that he lost sight of which way he was moving. Heaving with breath, his thighs screaming at their lactic threshold, Ryan stumbled down to his knees. He stared at the ground, thinking about collapsing into it, waiting to get buried with snow or debris, and just lie there until it all ended.

He reached down and looked at his compass. So turned around he had become, that he was now heading in the exact opposite direction from which he had started that morning. That course he was making so sure to stay on. Not that it mattered, for it was as likely as any to lead him somewhere useful, but it was more likely than running in circles, which he had now done for two days in a row. It was likely that he had negated all the hard work he had done before he started panicking.

Ryan leaned back to sit on his heels. For a moment he saw himself from above: head drooped, back sagging like an old man, no movement but blinking. All around him he saw the naked alders, as stark and confusing to his mind as a pack of zebras to lion. He stared deep into the forest, willing himself to be able to see their end. It wasn't like all vision just cut off in a wall around him. Somehow there had to be a direct line through the branches from the edge of the forest back to him. Ryan stared hard into the trees, almost willing his gaze to ignite a fire through them to lead him out.

Then, he suddenly realized that he was staring *at* something. One hundred yards away, and just emerging, there was something still, wooden, and camouflaged, but unnatural in its angles.

What was it?

The sight lured Ryan to his feet. He walked cautiously now, trying all along to figure out what he was looking at. Shorter stubs of wood, completely freed of bark stood in the distance. As he came closer, he realized that other beams traversed the stubs, which he now saw as about four feet high.

A fence! And just behind it was a clearing.

Ryan whooped and ran, jumping up in the air to lift his shouts higher. It was the presence of something man made, the knowledge that he wasn't in some part of the land so remote that he was the first human to ever see it, that brought his heart almost punching through his chest.

The area was in such disrepair that two things were immediately evident: no one was there, and there was still no protection from the bear. But somehow, just the presence of a spot that had lasted through the wilderness and elements was enough to give Ryan some hope.

When he reached the clearing, he received another shot of hope. There was a cabin. The logs had gaping holes between them where the mortar had long ago worn away, part of the roof looked like it had collapsed, but it was still recognizable and likely useful as a cabin.

As Ryan approached, he saw that it really was in deteriorating shape. There was a door, but it was opened inward and connected delicately by just the bottom hinge. Inside were photographs too yellowed to recognize anything more than eerie shapes—especially in the failing light. It was a mere six feet by eight feet, part of the roof was just gone, and the only piece of furniture was a handmade log chair. The floor was dirt, and over however many years pieces of leaves and drifts of snow had made their way in. The highlight, however, was an old pot-bellied stove that looked like it was still put together and a stack of old, split wood.

It wasn't perfect, by any means, but it was more than he could have imagined just a day ago. Ryan dropped his gear, then went outside and cut a sapling just the right size to sweep out the inside. With the area cleared, he went to work making the building more secure. He lifted the door and slid it into the frame, then wedged the chair behind it. A bear could still get it to open, but at least it would wake up Ryan along the way.

It was quiet all around him in the steadily darkening cabin. Just a little light came in through the hole in the ceiling a little more at the window. Once, Ryan had been out camping with his dad. He was in the tent alone and his dad had gone out exploring the area around them. Ryan had just been laying down when he heard a breath. Just a soft inhalation. But it was still a breath—cold and unmistakable. He was getting up to open the tent when all of the sudden he'd heard his father's voice shout, "Get outta here, bear! Get now!" and then what sounded like an ox trounce in the opposite direction. The point of the memory, he thought, is that, though a bear is big, and the cabin was surrounded by snow, the pads of a bear's feet were so soft and muffling, that it could be standing right outside the door without Ryan's knowing.

With slight unease in his mind, Ryan pulled the snowshoes off and settled them into a corner. He didn't want to start a fire until later when he really needed it. He pulled his sleeping bag out and stretched it across the floor, and settled in on top of it. He closed his eyes and tried to be aware of all sounds coming from outside the cabin. He was hoping to reach a stage of hyper-awareness, so that it would be long before the bear was huffing and puffing that Ryan knew he was there.

CHAPTER XIV

"The mountains are calling and I must go."

John Muir
(American naturalist and
founder of the Sierra Club

But it was a different sensation altogether that brought Ryan excitedly out of the sleep into which he had drifted: lights flashing across his eyelids. His eyes snapped open. There were lights, rising and falling.

"Here!" he shouted. "Here!"

Someone was looking for him. They were out there. Light was coming in through the hole in the ceiling and falling on his face. He raised his head to look out and saw streaks moving fluidly across the sky. He pushed up and rushed to the window cutout and saw that the lights in the horizon were changing colors.

Nature, it seemed, was putting on a light show for him. No one was out there searching. It was the Northern Lights, spinning and swirling like someone was dragging a spoon through the sky. He sat and watched them through the window until the amazement was pushed aside by the plummeting temperature, and Ryan knew he had to get a fire going.

He turned his attention to the outlines of the stove. It was time to see if the thing could still hold a fire. As best as he could tell, none of it seemed to have fallen into disrepair. Ryan felt through his pouch and located the flint and steel and the bag of kindling that was almost gone. He laid the piece of leather on the ground and put on the kindling, striking flames against it until it began to burn. Ryan lifted the fire like an offering and put the burning cotton balls into the fire. There were pieces of twigs and leaves on the floor that Ryan slowly added until they caught, then started putting the larger pieces from the stack inside the stove's belly.

The cast iron stove had an iron door that closed solidly. It would be easier to keep the fire going in there. In fact, the hardest part was getting it started. The heat and closed area would induce just about anything to burn.

Soon the stove was heating up nicely, and emanating off the walls and warming the entire room. Even some light was breaking from the stove. Puffs at a time, the stove began to belch smoke into the cabin. Ryan worried that the chimney might be blocked, but upon inspecting it he saw that the damper was not completely open. A little twist allowed a draft to pull the smoke up the stove pipe instead of pushing it into the cabin. Everything was working as planned.

With the fire spreading the warmth and safety all around him, Ryan laid back and continued watching the Aurora Borealis swathing the sky. The hole in the roof revealed that the cap on the place hadn't just been built out of wood, there was also a layer of tar paper built in with shingles on top. Ryan stood, reached out to it, and tore several pieces from the ceiling. It was brittle, but the composition of tar was still intact. He folded the paper and put it in his backpack.

Ryan pushed everything back in his bag and positioned it under his head as a pillow. It was the first time in a real shelter in quite a few nights. The fire was helping to relax him. But staring at the stove and watching the flickering made him wonder if his mother and father were staring into a fire as well, wondering if he was even still alive. In retrospect, he probably had beaten the odds with falling through the ice. More people likely died from that than lived through it.

The thoughts of falling through the ice followed him into his sleep. In those first minutes after he drifted off, he was under the water again. It was surrounding him, strangling the air out of his lungs, forbidding him from taking in more. He knew it was a dream and kept trying to make himself wake up, to take a full breath of air, but when he did, he was choking, coughing.

His eyes burst open for the second time that night. They immediately were stung by smoke in the air and started watering. Ryan squeezed them shut to clear them then opened them again. He covered his mouth with his hands and looked up at the stovepipe. It was glowing red hot like an angry totem pole. He had forgotten to turn the damper down to decrease the air flow and lower the fire. Fire was breaking through the pipe running up to the ceiling, and the wall behind it was starting to get licked by flames. Ryan watched in horror as the flames caught, spread, then seemed to surround him at every dry wall. The cabin had been standing for too long, was too dried out, and now it was burning down.

Ryan turned and pushed at the chair, but he had wedged in it too well—it was stuck. Maneuvering onto his back, Ryan dealt kicks to the underside of the chair, trying to knock it free. The first few pushed his back into the floor, then scraping along it backwards. Finally, the third and fourth kicks moved and dislodged the chair and the door fell open. Ryan crawled through it and away from the cabin.

Smoke poured through every crack and opening in the place. By the time he had pushed himself out, he couldn't even see his legs through the thick smoke. The blaze stretched onto the outside surfaces of the cabin.

Ryan suddenly realized that he'd made compounding mistakes. Not only had he started the fire, but he'd also left his pack inside the cabin. Survival was in the pack, and nowhere else. He would be completely helpless without it.

Wanting nothing more than to stay outside and regain his composure, Ryan made the decision to go back in and get it. More, he was compelled to do so. He wrenched his coat up around his head and dove back through the door. Immediately the heat was pushing unbearably on his whole body, even through the thick barrier of his coat. Ryan clutched blinding at the ground until he felt a strap. His fingers closed all around it and he leaned backwards, literally falling out of the cabin and rowing the bag on top of him.

It was sizzling hot, and embers were caught in the crevices and folds. Ryan rolled it in the snow until it was cool and cased in a thin sheen of white.

Suddenly a small, angry explosion came from the cabin. The fire must have reached the rifle and a bullet was discharging. Out here in the open, Ryan thought he could conceivably be shot by his own gun.

Pulling the bag, the boy crawled to a tree and sat with his back to it, between him and the fire. He thought he heard two or three other explosions of the rounds in the rifle going off.

His rifle and snowshoes were gone. Two massive hands of panic gripped and squeezed his throat. How would he protect himself from the wilderness? How would he move? If only a plane were flying by right now to see this wonderful signal fire that was all of his security and most of his hopes of survival turning to dust . . .

"Why?" Ryan cried out.

The shadows stretched out in front of him as the cabin burned neatly behind.

CHAPTER XV

*"The old Lakota was wise, He knew that man's heart,
away from nature, becomes hard; he know that lack of
respect for growing, living things soon led to lack of
respect for humans, too."*

Luther Standing Bear
(Native American author)

After a quarter of an hour or more had gone by without any explosions, Ryan circled around to the other side of the tree. The cabin was a giant ember that was beginning to die down. Under the heap, however, Ryan knew it was still hot. He was imagining the fastening straps of his snowshoes burned completely away, the hinged spikes red hot still and covered in soot.

Ryan curled around his bag. Luckily he'd managed to pull out his sleeping bag before it burned as well. The smell of smoke had seeped into all of them. The stench clogged his nostrils whenever he breathed.

There was no more sleep for him that night. That was obvious when the sun started to rise again and he was no closer to it than he was when he first realized the cabin was on fire. He should have been relieved to have survived yet again, but he was still so wound up about being in the clutches of danger, and disappointed about having lost nearly everything.

A warm Chinook wind was blowing down on him from the southwest. It wasn't warm enough to melt snow or warrant the removal of layers, but it was definitely a noticeable change. Ryan pulled his pack onto his back, took his bearings, and set out on foot again.

Whenever a complaint, objection, or second of self-pity dropped into his head, Ryan was careful to squash it away. It served nothing. There was no use in any of it. Nor did he let himself celebrate his victories. Too many times he had been burned—and it was always just when he was starting to feel like he was starting to do well. Of course, a rollercoaster has to go up before it can come down.

Well, the boy thought, no more of that for me. From now on, it's an even keel. I'll keep my head straight. No distractions for better or worse, because they always end up being for worse.

The snow was about a foot deep. Without snowshoes, he sunk down to the bottom with every step. It was hard going. The only thing that made it easier was that there was no end in sight—he was walking for the foreseeable future. Had he a destination he could count the steps, which would have made the trip even longer, the fatigue set in sooner. But at least with this he could just accept the pain and get on with it.

It did move him along more slowly, though.

People must be looking for him still. His walking stick had burned up in the fire, but he tried to remember how many days he'd notched in the thing. Six, he thought. Definitely six. So this was day seven. He made a mental note to devise some way to continue tracking the days. Somehow, he felt that, too, was important.

He just hoped he wasn't going in the wrong direction of everything. Hopefully that cabin was closer to a town than farther from it.

The long, slow day brought him through the alders and brush until the land opened into what seemed to be a large park. It was oddly shaped, but completely free of trees. Having learned his lesson well from the last time—and lacking a stick to test the composition of the ground in front of him—Ryan stuck close to the tree line all along what could have been a meadow or water hole.

The food was officially gone. The granola bar was gone, the dried moose meat was all eaten. Maybe that stick wouldn't have gotten too many more notches, he thought. There's not too many ways to coax food out of a frozen wilderness—especially with no fishing or hunting supplies around.

Ryan stopped and shouted into the air, "Why do I deserve this?"

He had images of himself, stomach shrunk in and ribs jutting out of tight skin beneath his coat, lying in a field, too weak to move on.

Had he the energy for it, he probably would have sinking spirits.

"Why?" he shouted again, louder.

And this time a voice came back to him.

"What's that? Who's there?" he shouted again.

The voice came back again. And this time he heard it. It was his voice inside saying, "Life is what it is."

And the voice was right. Life is a day at a time, a chance to stand against a challenge. It was his. Even with the circumstances he was in, it was his.

The thought, though empowering, wasn't enough to make him want to build another fire, another shelter. Not when he had no food, no gun, no decent shoes for travelling. But that was the point, he supposed, that whatever power he still had to control his own end, he would have to do it.

He chose a spot between two trees, just on the edge of the clearing. It wasn't quite evening, but he knew he would travel no more. The clearing was good because it gave him an opportunity to make himself visible if something arrived, but still have shelter and fuel for a fire. For better or worse, he decided he was married to this place from here on. There was no energy left to travel with no food. He had arrived to where he would be rescued or where he would . . .

The Chinook winds were dying down. He needed to start a fire, get his shelter going. He chose first to gather wood, then to clear his fire base. He would start the fire later, but wanted to have these mundane, time consuming details out of the way before he actually needed the fire. He cleared some ground for the fire base, and rounded up all the wood he could find nearby. He even scavenged some extra to use as a signal fire if needed, and cleared an even larger platform for that fire. It would need to be huge and fast when the time came.

He then set to work harvesting the young spruce boughs to create a bed, then the larger ones to create a lean-to between two trees. The fire base was between the trees, so he left his lean-to's opening toward the fire. He had quite a few extra boughs, so he set to work in creating a fire shield. He had heard the idea of one before, and being in the cabin reminded him of it the night before. Essentially it was a wall behind the fire that pushed the heat back toward him, rather than letting it escape into the night.

Soon, when everything was in place, Ryan created the fire that would provide him the warmth he needed through the night. Between the lean to behind him, the fire in front of him, and the shield on the other side, he found that he warmed up quite nicely. He looked down at the flint and steel connected by the leather shoe lace and realized that this was the tool that had saved his life to this point.

He decided to continue gathering firewood for the signal fire. It was best to stay busy now.

CHAPTER XVI

"All living creatures and all plants are a benefit to something."

Okute (Sioux Indian)

Contrast is the name of the game in signaling. The real challenge, however, was in making sure that he could provide that contrast, no matter what the circumstance. After piling more wood reserves than he hoped to ever need, Ryan settled into his lean-to. Night was easy: a big, bright fire. Daytime was trickier. He had a mirror that he could use to signal, but he was unsure that he could hit a plane from a far distance with it. Though the idea was good—light coming from the ground rather than the sun is a contrast to the expected, training a light on an object at distance is harder than it might seem in the movies. Plus, what if it was cloudy? What then? Hopefully the pilot would notice the smoke, but what if it didn't provide enough contrast? What if the clouds were low? Ryan played through the many scenarios in his mind.

After awhile he decided to ready everything. Preparedness was in his control. He went to the signal fire area out in the open, snow covered meadow and stacked the dried logs and limbs in a teepee design. He left a gap open so that in a rush he could scoop the hot coals from his fire with a concave chunk of bark and dump them inside, igniting the dried timber and sending its smoke into the air quickly, or—in case it was night—provide enough light to draw the attention of the pilot.

Overall the plan was a good one. He would just need to execute it when the time came.

Ryan sat and tried to think of all the things his dad had told him. Why hadn't he listened more? His dad had all sorts of bits of information he'd picked up in life. Too bad Ryan hadn't bothered to acquire that knowledge. Of course, he was acquiring his own, now . . .

And then the thoughts began falling like dominoes. The gun, the food, the loneliness. All of it was weighing down on him. He was getting tired of being down, it was literally draining what little energy reserves he had left. He needed to beat the challenges of Mother Nature, not get beat down by the challenges of negativity.

On the drive up from Texas the family had suffered two flat tires. It seemed especially hard on his mother, who was particularly worried that no one had a job and money was a finite thing. They had savings, yes, but not a house, or income, or extra money to be spending on tires or other repairs.

"PMA," his dad told her. "PMA, Positive Mental Attitude, we gotta have it." It was another of his mantras.

It came back to Ryan now—*PMA, PMA . . .*

Then a sound came out of the woods behind him. Chimes? It sounded like the chimes again. Could the bear have followed him here?

His mood—which had just been turning up—was dashed away by the panic. He was the bear's next meal. He knew it was out there. Ryan had flushed himself out of the cabin—the best shot he had at a modicum of protection. And now the bear was tracking him, following him, and finally here.

The gun was gone. All Ryan had was the fire. He stacked more wood on it, hoping to make it big enough that it would scare the bear away. The center burned a hot blue. If he needed to he could grab pieces that were half lit and throw them, anything to keep the bear at bay.

Ryan sat and forced himself to be calm. The sound, what had he heard? Was it his imagination? It was certainly a sound. But he couldn't be sure what he heard.

The shadows were getting long around him. It was still clearly a part of day, but the sun was starting to make its circle back down on the horizon. Maybe one hour of daylight remained.

Then a new sound slipped in from the horizon. Not the chimes, not the bear. Two seconds later he realized it was the motor of a plane! Someone was nearby! Near enough to hear! No mistakes, he knew he had to get this one right. Ryan jerked himself up out and set to action.

He scooped some of the reddening chunks of wood out of the fire and brought them over to the signaling area. He made a second trip and picked up more. Soon the fire was blazing. He could still hear the sound of the motor, but for the moment it didn't seem to be getting any closer or further away. He feared it would, though.

Ryan looked up into the sky. It was too bright, the smoke too light. It probably all blended in together. He needed contrast. The smoke wasn't enough. What could he do? White smoke from a fire against the white snow covered ground would not yield much contrast.

The tar paper! Suddenly he remembered the tar paper he had pulled off the cabin. He rushed to his bag, threw everything out until he found the two large, folded squares. With both of them in his hands, Ryan began to twist them into cylinders that he hoped would burn the quickest and release the most smoke. The rolled up ends jammed directly into the fire, and seconds later a thick, black smoke began to rise from the pile.

"See me, see me . . ." Ryan was willing to himself, listening to the motor turning.

Plumes of dark smoke continued rising as if one mass. Suddenly the sound of the motor sputtered, a brief reduction in power. It was on purpose. The pilot had seen the signal and was coming to search the area!

The engine grew louder and Ryan was shouting and jumping. The frozen tundra was awakened by a blast of 14-year old screaming, which actually seemed to outshout the engine of the place.

The plane flew low into the clearing, close enough that Ryan could see the bolts in the undercarriage. The pilot tipped the wing, as though lifting a hat and saying, "Good day!"

"YEEEAAHHH!" Ryan shouted out.

Finally, Ryan had made it.

CHAPTER XVII

"The earth, like the sun, like the air,
belongs to everyone—and to no one."

Edward Abbey
(American writer and naturalist)

The plane circled the snow covered park once again. Ryan stood in awe. The pilot slowly glided through the air toward him. The skis of the plane exploded the untouched snow as Mac taxied and slid to a stop. He cut the engine and the door flew open. The ordeal was over. Ryan Larsen was now a survivor. He was a survivor of one of the harshest environments on the face of the earth. All the fear, anxiety, and tension of the last six days drained away leaving him numb. He ran toward the plane, tears freezing on his cheeks. The last battle was won, the war was over. He gasped for air as if he had just run hundreds of yards in deep snow. Frozen in the moment, he saw three people jump from the plane. The pilot, his mom, and his dad all had come to greet the young explorer.

All of the lessons he had learned had served him well and he felt overwhelmed by the moment. Ryan's dad was the first to reach him although his mom was there just seconds later. It was like a marathon runner finishing an uphill race, his emotional trials coupled with the physical strain and lack of food had totally emptied his energy supplies. He was spent.

Everyone was crying and laughing and talking at the same time. Ryan had so many emotions running through his young mind. Like anyone who gets lost, he felt guilty and felt like he'd done something wrong. He began to apologize to his parents, but his dad quickly stopped him. Bill was so happy that they had finally found Ryan alive and unhurt, he wanted to just enjoy the moment. Talking and explaining would come later.

While Ryan and his parents were getting used to the idea that he had been found, Mac gathered Ryan's gear and stuffed it in the back of the plane. He hollered, "Let's get going. The weather is closing in and we don't want to miss our window of opportunity to get airborne."

Everyone hurried to the plane and stepped up into the cabin. The pilot fired up the engine and turned into the wind. As they roared across the snow, Ryan simply looked out of the window. His mind still racing, he wondered where the wolves and bear had gone. Were they listening to the plane taking off? Thinking back over the past week he realized that he had fulfilled his objective. He learned about himself, he learned that he was self-reliant, and he had most certainly learned about the power of the wilderness and lessons it had to teach. Regardless of where they were or what they were thinking, Ryan Larsen was glad to be going back home.

The flight was going to take about twenty minutes, so the pilot only climbed to about 1000 feet. The wind was tricky at that altitude. The plane tossed and bounced on air currents, but nothing could scare Ryan at this point. His nerves had already been worn down to the nub. Ryan's parents respected his silence and remained quiet, enjoying just the sight of him sitting next to them. His mom reached her hand out to clutch his and held on tight. She felt the relief of touching her only child. Tears welled up in her eyes once again as she closed her eyes in thankful prayer. Her prayers had indeed this day been answered.

The pilot tipped the wings of the plane to take a look at his landing site and the weather vane showing him wind direction. After lining up, he knew the landing would be with a cross wind. He really had no choice since he had only one landing strip. He skillfully cut the engine and adjusted his flaps for a soft and uneventful landing. The plane cut through the snow with ease as he taxied up to the Larsen's truck.

"Thank you for finding me, Mr. Stewart," Ryan said.

Mac smiled and answered, "My pleasure, Ryan."

After a short pause, Ryan continued, "I was wondering if it was really going to happen, but I did keep the faith that someone would come."

With a parent on each side of him, Ryan walked to the truck, threw his pack into the back and climbed into the cab to head for home.

THE END

Edwards Brothers Malloy
Ann Arbor MI. USA
June 30, 2016